This 1989 edition published by Derrydale Books,
distributed by Crown Publishers, Inc.,
225 Park Avenue South
New York, N.Y. 10003

Directed by HELENA Productions Ltd.
Illustrated by Van Gool-Lefevre-Loiseaux

Produced by Twin Books
15 Sherwood Place
Greenwich, CT 06830

Printed and bound in Spain

ISBN 0-517-69316-X

hgfedcba

Printed in Spain by
Printer industria gráfica sa. Barcelona
D. L. B.: 26787-1989

The Emperor's New Clothes

DERRYDALE BOOKS
New York

Twin Books

Once, long ago, there lived an emperor who had a great fondness for beautiful clothes. He cared so much about his wardrobe that he had more tailors than soldiers. He attended every social event, and sometimes invented new ones, just to show off his latest fashions. In fact, he had a different outfit for every hour of the day. And he demanded so much flattery that his advisors had little time for anything else.

The emperor's subjects spent half their time attending parades and processions instead of getting their daily work done.

8

But the emperor didn't realize what his vanity was costing the nation. He went right on strutting proudly through the streets in his ever-changing costumes.

The empire's capital city was large and beautiful. Visitors came from far away to see its sights—giving the emperor still more excuses for parades and parties.

His tailors had to work around the clock to keep up with his demands for new finery.

11

The emperor's dressing room was as big as the ballroom of his palace. Every morning, he looked over the rows of magnificent robes, capes, and crowns to choose a wardrobe for the day's events. His servants waited anxiously outside the door for his decisions.

One day, two strangers appeared in the city: a fox named Needle and a monkey, who called himself Thread. They claimed to be master tailors from a faraway country who had come to weave the emperor a set of clothes whose beauty would be unmatched in all the world. In fact, the strangers were swindlers, but news of their coming soon reached the emperor.

14

15

When they arrived at the palace, Needle and Thread bowed graciously to the emperor.

"Your majesty," they said, "the marvelous cloth we weave has colors and patterns undreamed of in your realm. Not only that—it has the magical quality of being invisible to anyone who is stupid or unfit for his office."

"How wonderful!" thought the emperor. "Beauty and wisdom combined!"

"Begin your work at once," he ordered.

After receiving a huge sum of
money with which to buy
materials, Needle and Thread set
up their loom and began to pretend
they were weaving.

All the fine silver and gold thread they had demanded was hidden away in their room. But the sound of their empty loom was heard in the palace far into the night. Everyone was impressed with their hard work.

19

The emperor was bursting with curiosity about the progress of his new clothes. Finally, he sent his elderly prime minister, Sir Leonine, to see how the work was coming along. Poor Sir Leonine was shocked to find that he couldn't see the cloth displayed so proudly by the weavers! "I must be unfit for my office," he thought humbly. "But I will pretend I can see."

Unwilling to lose the emperor's confidence, Sir Leonine returned to the throne room with a glowing report. "The work is progressing magnificently, Sire. Such patterns! Such colors! It must be seen to be believed."

The emperor was thrilled.

"Spare no expense in supplying the master tailors with everything they require," he ordered. And a steady stream of servants passed into the workroom with bolts of raw silk, spools of glittering metallic thread, and yards of expensive trimming. The two swindlers put all this into their hiding place and continued their pretense of weaving.

Word spread all over the city. "The master tailors are making the emperor's new clothes so magnificent that there will be a national holiday to see them in a great procession!"

26

Finally, the emperor could stand the suspense no longer. He went to the workroom himself. Imagine his shock and surprise when he couldn't see the beautiful cloth held up before him!

"Great heavens!" he thought. "Am I stupid? Am I unfit to be emperor? How is it that I can't see the cloth?"

But, of course, he pretended to see it. "*Magnifique!*" he cried delightedly.

The emperor was so anxious to conceal his dullness that he called a great assembly and bestowed upon the two imposters the newly created Order of Master Tailor to the Empire!

Once their "weaving" was finished, Needle and Thread pretended to cut the cloth and fit it to a tailor's dummy. The townspeople gathered outside the workroom window to marvel at the beauty of the cloth and the elegant cut of the emperor's new clothes. No one was willing to admit that he couldn't see a thing, lest his neighbors think him stupid.

When the clever swindlers had finished their cutting act, the emperor was called in for fittings. Turning this way and that in his undershirt, he tried in vain to catch even a glimpse of his new clothes. Meanwhile, Needle and Thread kept up a steady stream of admiring chatter as they pretended to measure, tuck, and pin.

At last, the long-awaited day arrived. A special canopy was lifted high above the emperor. The master tailors took their places behind him, pretending to hold up the long trailing train of his rich new robe. Clutching his sceptre nervously, and clad only in his undershirt, the emperor led off the procession.

The townspeople lined the streets in high excitement and cheered when they saw the canopy approaching.

The emperor's subjects applauded loudly and shouted their approval as he paced solemnly along. "What a magnificent robe! And the train! Never has our emperor been so splendidly dressed!"

But suddenly, a small clear voice was heard above the noise of the crowd. "Daddy," said the voice in a tone of wonder, "the emperor has no clothes on!"

Embarrassed, the father tried to quiet the child. "Don't be silly," he whispered. But the child repeated his words in a louder tone, and the crowd took them up: "The emperor has no clothes on!"

Everyone was so glad that he
didn't have to pretend anymore
that the whole crowd burst into
roars of laughter.

At last, even the emperor burst out laughing! He laughed at his own silliness and at the cleverness of Needle and Thread. He laughed at the silliness of his subjects and courtiers, who had been so afraid of looking foolish that they pretended to see what wasn't there. And the master tailors laughed hardest of all—because they had shown that it was more fun to admit you were silly together than to pretend you were wise alone.